Katie Fry
PRIVATE EYE

The Missing Fox

Written by Katherine Cox
illustrated by Vanessa Brantley Newton

SCHOLASTIC INC.

ISBN 978-0-545-66675-6

10 9 8 7   18 19/0

Printed in the U.S.A.   40
First printing 2015

Book design by Maria Mercado

Chapter One

This is Katie and Sherlock.

and Sherlock
Let Katie Solve
Your Mysteries!

Free!
(No Refunds)

Katie has a big brain.
Sherlock has a big appetite.
They are best friends, and they both love
to solve mysteries.

They solved the mystery of the missing snack.

They solved the mystery of the misplaced purse.

They even solved the mystery of the trashed trashcans.

Conclusion:

Someone Keeps opening the gate

Trash bags are ripped open

All the food scraps are gone.

Katie and Sherlock want a new mystery.
One they have to leave the yard to solve.

"We have a case for you," Mom calls from the front door.
"Good enough," says Sherlock.

9

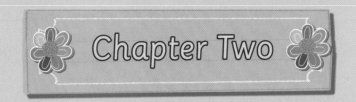

Chapter Two

Katie and Sherlock know what to do.
First they find out what the mystery is.
"It's Fox," says Matt "He's missing!"
"We need to gather all the witnesses," Katie says.

Dad looks around the room.
"Done," he says.

Katie asks questions and writes down clues.
"What did Fox do today?" she asks Matt.
"This morning he was the lifeguard on duty at the pool," says Matt.
That is all Matt can remember.

"This might be our toughest case yet,"
Sherlock says. He can't remember what
they are looking for.
"You can count on us to find Fox,"
Katie tells Matt.

Katie and Sherlock check the pool for clues.

"He was here all right," Sherlock says.
"But he's gone now," Katie says.

Katie and Sherlock keep looking.
Fox's trail leads them to the library.

Sherlock checks out a book.
Katie checks for clues. She finds a pair of Fox's
spaceman goggles, but no Fox.

Katie and Sherlock look for Fox in the kitchen.
They find lunch instead.

Katie thinks and thinks about the case.
Sherlock thinks about his sandwich.

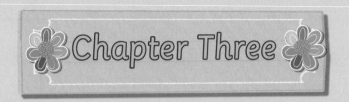

Chapter Three

Katie looks over her clues, and makes note of the goggles.
"Where did you and Fox play spaceman?" Katie asks Matt.
"The tree house," he says.

Missing

They all run to the backyard.

Sherlock gets a bird's-eye view.

"Have you seen a spaceman?" Sherlock asks the squirrel.
"He was hard to miss. The little guy suffered a really rough landing. No goggles," the squirrel says.

"No landing pad either," Katie says.
"It was here earlier!" her brother swears. "Look!"

There is no sign of Fox anywhere.
Katie uses her big brain to think.

"I've got it!" Katie says.

Chapter Four

"Stop!" Katie calls to Dad. "Don't move that box."
"We are giving all of this away," Dad says.

"Not all of it," Katie says. "This morning, you brought this box to the backyard to collect our old toys. Fox used it as a landing pad. He's been there the whole time."

"Fox!" Sherlock and Matt yell.

"Great job solving the case," Mom says.
"How would you like to celebrate?" Dad asks.

Katie smiles. "One more playtime before we say good-bye to our old things?"